KIM DEAL & ME

4 STORIES

ALSO BY RYAN FORSYTHE

FICTION

*Dick Cheney Saves Paris:
a personal and political madcap sci-fi meta- anti- novel*

If You Don't Read This The Terrorists Will Win

ART

Slugdala! 13 Banana Slug Mandalas

*The Doodle, Design, & Draw Book
for Illinois Valley Kids of All Ages*

CHILDREN'S BOOKS
FOR ADULTS

The Little Veal Cutlet That Couldn't

*Goldilocks and the Three BARs
(Beyond Available Resources)*

AS EDITOR

*Cobra Lily: a Review of Southwest Oregon
Literature and Art (Volumes 1-5)*

KIM DEAL & ME

4 STORIES*

* Not all about Kim, but to be fair, all do interrelate

Kim Deal & Me: 4 Stories
Copyright © 2019 Ryan Forsythe

Initially published as e-book only, August 2013

Cover design by Paul Forristal

Back cover photograph by Archana (with Ryan's camera) taken the night of the Breeders show

ISBN 978-1-945824-29-6
First Left Fork Print Edition: August 2019

2 4 6 8 9 7 5 3 1

Published by Left Fork
PO Box 110
O'Brien, OR 97534
www.leftfork.org

Printed in the United States of America

*Dedicated to the Winter 1994 term
English 265 class at Ohio State,
most notably Brendon, Jerry, and Jenny,
but also Amie, Amy, Brian, other Brian,
Cinnamon, Dagfinn, Dan, Erik, Greg, James,
Huei-Chen, Paul, Renee, and Sarah.
And oh heck...for Judy too.*

*Also to Bob and Archana:
Thanks for joining me on the Quest.*

*And to Kim, Kelley, Jim, and Josephine:
I know you're a real coo coo.*

Contents

KIM DEAL & ME

4 STORIES

Author's Note

Somewhere, most likely Twitter or Facebook the way news travels these days, I learned that the Breeders were planning a 20th anniversary tour and re-release of *Last Splash*. To me, twenty years since the album means twenty years since the tour in support of the album. And that means twenty years since the fated show at the Newport in Columbus when I arrived with a story in my back pocket and a goal to get it to Kim Deal.

A few months earlier, for my first creative writing class, I turned in a story about two guys who drive to Dayton, Ohio, in search of their favorite rock star. The class loved "Slack and Me and the Quest for Kim Deal"; the teacher...not so much. Being the naive young cocksure writer that I was, of course I followed up with "Writer's Block," an all too thinly veiled critique of said teacher. And then for a class the next year, I wrote "Five Years and You're Out," a personal essay detailing (among other things) the writing of that story ("Writer's Block") about the writing of the first story ("Slack and Me...").

No, not all four stories are about Kim Deal, though all four do interconnect. In fact, the way it's structured, two of the stories function something as tangents from the essay. And yes, the bulk of what follows was written for two of my first creative writing classes ever, some twenty-years ago. Needless to say, I won't vouch for the quality of the writing, though I do believe it's a quick and fun read.

Hard to believe it's going on two decades, but hey, if Kim and Co. are celebrating, then I too can commemorate the moment when I wrote a story about a quest to find Kim Deal and then decided I should undertake my own quest to get her the story.

-Ryan
August 2013

Five Years and You're Out

Five minutes into my first biology class at The Ohio State University, I stopped taking notes.

I was pretty sure I had heard the professor clearly, but I wanted to make sure, so I turned to the person seated next to me. "Excuse me, but did she just say 'in fact' three times in the same sentence?"

"I think so," he said. "Maybe it's some kind of rare genetic disorder."

We started keeping a record of each and every time she uttered the soon-to-be-annoying phrase. We could hardly believe our tally sheet as the bell rang on that first class. Not counting the five minutes before we noticed her bizarre practice, Dr. Elizabeth Gross said "in fact" over sixty times.

We probably wouldn't have noticed, if she hadn't tossed it into her sentences in places where it just didn't fit. "During, in fact, chemi-osmosis in chloroplasts, light, via electron transports in fact, produces a hydrogen ion gradient, which can, in fact, produce ATP in the dark."

As we filed out of class, we discussed Dr. Gross's "in fact" fetish. In particular, we were curious as to whether she would maintain her pace or whether she was getting them out of her system for the whole quarter. Having only the experience of one lecture to draw from, we decided the issue required further investigation. For the rest of the quarter, we would chart every "in fact." Somewhere in there, he introduced himself as Norm.

Every biology lecture passed in the same manner, with Norm and I collecting our "in facts." We each kept an independent account of the day's activity (to control for error). At the end of class, we would compare notes, the official total for the day being the average of our two, rounded down. After a few days we added color commentary, for the entertainment of those who sat around us.

"That's four times in one minute, Norm. What are the odds of her hitting the century mark today?"

"At that rate, Ryan, it won't be difficult. But I don't think she can maintain it. It appears as though she's getting tired. Keep in mind that we have a video coming up later in class. That will further cut into her time."

"I have to disagree," I would reply. "The video is going to be a catalyst. It'll allow her to catch her breath, and then look out, class, as she comes back stronger than ever!"

There was one time a student told us to be quiet, but those around us told him to move if he didn't want to listen.

Once every lecture or two, Dr. Gross would look up from her overhead, sensing that someone in the sea of faces before her was talking, and advise the class not to disrupt her lecture.

Norm and I felt unappreciated by that. The way we saw it, we were providing a service. The dry ramblings of her uninspiring lecture certainly were not bringing students to class. If our comic relief kept just one student from walking out of class, I think Dr. Gross should have thanked us.

Instead, she glared at the class, and bellowed, "If you feel you don't need the lecture, you can leave now. In fact, get out now, whoever you are."

As it was a huge lecture hall, and we sat near the back, we knew she couldn't identify who was, in fact, mocking her. Norm and I would continue.

"That's thirty-seven so far today, Norm. I still say she can do it."

It only took five lectures before she hit one hundred, and she did it with ten minutes left in class. It was October 7, 1993. She was probably excited because the subject of the day's lecture was Chapter Four: Cells. Before the day was out Dr. Gross set what Norm and I believe had to be some sort of record for most times saying "in fact" in one lecture. One hundred-nineteen stinkin' times. We realized that there was no way to confirm if this was indeed the all-time record for all schools nationwide—probably records were never kept before Dr. Gross—but Norm and I still considered it the unofficial record.

As we continued to keep the statistics, we tried to keep our routine from getting as monotonous as Dr. Gross. We started taking predictions from those around us. Whoever was closest each day without going over received the right to make the first prediction the following lecture (this was important because no two people were allowed to make the same forecast). Once the people behind me bet money on the total.

"She's going to set the record today, Man. I can feel it!"

"No way, Dude. She's not even going to hit eighty."

"Betcha three bucks?"

"Alright. You're on."

Dr. Gross didn't set the record that day. In fact, she didn't come within thirty of her high for the rest of the time she taught us. I do have the statistics. Her total was 692.0 times during eleven lectures, for a mean of 62.91, and a median of 56.0. The range was 17.0-119.0, with a standard deviation of 28.19. These statistics don't include the midterm examination where she only spoke for two minutes.

These numbers were my fuel for teacher evaluations. "How can we expected to get anything out of a class where the instructor herself can not get past two little words?" I wrote. I then provided the stats, including the most in one solitary sentence (six).

Those who sat around me always complained about these lectures. I felt sorry for them and the others who were there and actually wanted to learn something. I, too, would have been disappointed if I was trying to get something from it. I knew better than to expect anything, though; by that point, I had already been in college for two years.

I guess it was my second quarter when I began souring to the whole higher education concept. I was taking an honors course in mathematics when I discovered the inability of a professor to communicate with the students.

After working on the same problem for ten minutes, Monique Vuillemier was getting tired and the chalkboard was nearing capacity. Rather than chalk up the board with every little step, she started doing it in her head, maybe writing every third or fourth step down. As she wasn't telling us the in-between steps, we all wondered how she got from step six to step nine. One student dared ask the question.

"In the steps on the left side there—"

"Which left side?" Monique asked. I always wondered about that one.

"The fifth line down," said the student. "How do you know to go from that, to what you have in the next line?"

"What do you mean, how do I know?" snapped Monique. "Of course I know—I've been teaching math for twenty years! Silly question!"

She said it in such a way that it sounded more like, "Insolent boy!" If she was closer, I think she would have asked him to stick out his hands before rapping them with a ruler.

We never did figure out how she made the leaps in logic. We didn't care, though; we were all busy daydreaming of the last day of the quarter, when we would leave Monique forever. Before the ten weeks had passed, however, we received our schedules for Spring Quarter. Next to Mathematics H263, was her name. Naturally, we all wanted to change sections of the course, but investigation revealed that only one section of the class would be taught. If we wanted to take Math H263, we had no choice but Monique.

Looking back, I wonder why I wanted to. Why

was my desire to take the class greater than my need to escape Monique Vuillemier? But I know why I did it.

A few years earlier, during my junior year in high school, I had taken the PSAT, one of those standardized tests that supposedly measures how well the person will do in college. Based on my performance on an exam that I took on one sun-shiny Saturday morning in March of that year, I came into college with a designation as an "Honors" student.

Even before I took a class, academic counselors began hounding me to take classes that supposedly had a higher degree of difficulty. During summer orientation, when I was scheduling classes for my first quarter, my advisor encouraged me in the way of honors courses. "Honors classes are wonderful because you meet with actual professors, rather than graduate students," noted Rosemary Gliem. "Also, class sizes are limited, so you get to know your classmates."

So far I was interested. "But aren't they harder?" I asked.

"Instructors take into account the fact that it is an honors class. Whereas the average grade in a regular course is a 'C,' in honors courses the average grade is generally a 'B.' Many students find they do their best work in these classes as they are motivated to work harder."

Anything else?

"Also, if you successfully complete an Honors Contract, indicating that you will be pursuing a rigorous course of study, you will have 'with Honors' inscribed on your diploma."

I was an easy sell. If the instructors took the difficulty into account come grade time, I had no problem taking a more challenging course load. Plus, I'd have a diploma that said "with Honors." That would be cool. And so, I signed up for thirty-six hours of honors courses my freshman year.

One such honors course was Sarah Boysen's introductory psychology class. If there was a bad instructor Olympics, Sarah Boysen would challenge Dr. Gross for the gold.

At first her class wasn't so bad. The first day, she did not spend any time going over the syllabus, explaining her policies, et cetera. Instead, she informed us of a paper that we would have to do. "The only thing that really differentiates you guys from people in the regular version is that, while they will be subjects in an experiment, you will actually be designing an experiment in a fifteen page paper." That sounded somewhat interesting, designing our own experiment.

"In fact," Professor Boysen continued. "I think this paper is so important that if you do really well on it, I will drop your lowest of the two midterm examinations." Wow! I usually did pretty well on papers—exams were my weakness—and she was saying she would drop one of the two exams for the quarter. I worked on the paper for weeks to make it as perfect as I could; I had no doubt that I would need to have one of those exams dropped. All my work paid off when I received the paper back with a solid "A" circled on the top of the cover. Throughout the eighteen pages of my research paper on lie detector tests, she had marked only one other thing. On the last page, she wrote: "Great Paper!"

When she described the format for her exams, I was thankful that one exam would not count against me. "The exams will include short answer, matching, true/false, and essay components." That meant I really had to know the material; I couldn't just find the answer amongst three or four other choices, like on the old multiple-choice exam. I spent the days leading up to the first exam, memorizing the book. I pulled through with an eighty-six percent, not stellar, but certainly respectable. I wanted to do better on the second exam, so I could guarantee myself a high grade in the class. I spent countless hours going over all the information that her T.A. had provided during the seven or eight lectures that Sarah Boysen couldn't make (we only had twenty lectures, by the way). All that time and effort produced a second eighty-six percent.

I don't know what I was expecting, but when my grades showed up and I saw the flat "B" next to Psychology H100, I was disappointed. Hadn't she said she'd drop an exam? Now I was a math major the quarter before, and as far as I could tell, an eighty-six and an A/Great paper! averaged to more than a "B."

I called her up to voice my concern.

"What were all your grades?" she asked.

"I received eighty-six percent on each of the exams," I replied. "On the paper, all you wrote on the entire thing was 'A! Great paper!'"

"And what grade did you get in the class?"

"I received a 'B,'" I answered.

"And, tell me, what were you expecting?"

I could tell this was not going to be a happy conversation. I explained that, given that she had mentioned dropping one of the exams, I assumed she would have averaged the eighty-six and the "A" and come up with at the very very least, a "B+," but more likely an "A-", and possibly an "A" depending on the strength of the paper. I wasn't looking for special treatment; I just wanted her to live up to her promise.

"First of all," she began. "I don't care much for pluses and minuses. I don't think they are useful."

While I disagreed with her, I could accept this much. I thought I should have had an A, not an A minus or B plus. I wanted to know what kept me from the solid "A."

"Second of all, you didn't have a lower exam."

What?

"Did you just say what I thought you said?" She had. She explained that the first day of class she did say she would drop the lower exam grade. I, however, didn't have a lower exam grade; they were both eighty-six percent. I came close to exploding.

"Do you mean to tell me, that if I hadn't studied at all, that if I completely blew off one of the exams, and ended up with a forty percent on that last exam, I would have a higher grade now because you would have dropped it and averaged the A with one eighty-six?"

Although I shouldn't have been too surprised by her answer, I must admit I truly was.

"Well, those are pretty good grades," she said. "I wouldn't think that you'd want me to drop one."

Ten minutes later we were still arguing. After I hung up the phone, I began drafting a letter to the dean of psychology, the president of the university, whoever would hear my plight. I never sent it though. Having just switched to psychology from a business major, I was intimidated by the prospect of making enemies and being labeled a troublemaker this early on in my newfound field.

Besides, I was starting to get used to such treatment.

The same quarter I listened to Dr. Gross spew "in facts," I found myself sitting in Paul Greblo's abnormal psychology class two days a week.

Every day, we were surprised to learn that he had started lecture. The gray monotone of the man we called the "Human Barbiturate" could not be discerned from the natural pre-bell murmur of zippers unzipped and notebooks flipped open to clean pages. I was usually updating those next to me on Dr. Gross's prolific day.

I took notes during the first lecture, and again during the second, and to an extent during the third and fourth, as well. I didn't have to for the fifth. In reading the textbook, I discovered that the lecture I listened to Tuesdays and Thursdays from 2:30 until 4:00 pm was a summary of the book. For the next few classes, I paid careful attention to the lecture and verified at home each night that we had been given an outline of the chapter.

The students who sat next to me didn't realize this, so I thought I'd have some fun. Before the next class, I outlined the chapter myself.

"Hey, guys. Bet I can predict everything our teacher says today."

They were amazed when they saw Paul Greblo read my notes to us. Perhaps I shouldn't have done this. As soon as they realized what Paul was up to, half the class stopped showing up. If the classroom wasn't on my way home as I walked back from biology, I probably wouldn't have stopped in either. I knew some people in the class who had a thirty-minute commute, before having to find a parking space. Listening to our instructor read what they had read the night before or would be reading the following night or in four weeks on the night before the exam wasn't too helpful for them. So they stopped showing up. He held it against us.

"If no one wants to show up for class and learn the material, then why should I give you the benefit of the doubt," he said after the particularly difficult midterm examination. "Forty-six people showed up to take the exam. On any other day less than twenty people show up. It's clear to me that you guys don't care about the material and don't care about your grades, so I'm not going to curve the exam."

The exam was a fifty-question, multiple-choice test, which supposedly tested our knowledge enough to count for fifty percent of the quarter grade. Miss one question, miss a percent.

Like most people, there are questions that I am almost positive on and others that I just have to guess.

I was surprised as we went over the exam to find the ones I wasn't sure of marked correct and some of the ones I was sure of marked wrong.

Something was not right. I was sure of those answers—after all, I had read the book myself and heard it read by Paul Greblo as well. I approached him about the ones that had been marked wrong. He listened to me as I argued for my answers, nodding his head in agreement.

"I can see how you could have interpreted the questions as you did. They were kind of vague and certainly could have been read the way you read them. I'm not going to give you the points, however. You have to keep in mind that everyone gets the same questions, so it wouldn't be fair to give you the points."

Huh?

I debated with him for the next ten minutes, using every argument I could come with but to no success. He remained firm: he wasn't going to curve it (because no one showed up because he was reading the book to them and they didn't want to waste three hours of their life getting to and from hearing him read the book) and he wasn't going to give me the extra points (because even though he agreed with my interpretation of the questions and that with my interpretation my answers would be 100% correct, it wouldn't be fair to others in the class because they had been given the same [unfair] test).

For my first few years, stories of crummy professors, unfair examinations, and painful lectures were the norm. I wondered if this was really the norm at the university, or whether my college career had just gotten off to a wretched start. If it was just that the dandruff from the proverbial noggin of academia had fallen on my shoulders, it would be unfair to criticize the overall quality of instruction. If there were quality instructors hiding somewhere, I could only blame myself for not spending my free time snooping for them. In light of this, when the beginning of my third year rolled around, I made up my mind to do something about my dissatisfaction. I began "The Quest."

My mission throughout all of fall quarter: to find one professor who could at the very least stimulate me enough to stay awake through a lecture, but more hopefully, one who could encourage and educate me, provoke me, inspire and incite me to reach that untapped potential that I felt existed deep within, but as of yet, had not been prodded.

With this objective in mind, I interrogated everyone I knew.

"Now, I'm going to ask you some questions," I would begin. "I want you to take this seriously and answer as truthfully as you can. Don't feel rushed, take your time and think about this before you respond. Have you, or anyone you know, ever taken a class with a decent professor, someone you would actually *recommend* to others?"

A few said their instructors had been okay, but most people were not very positive. Oh sure, they weren't completely down on their professors, but with comments the likes of "this professor was not bad," "I wasn't disappointed by that one," or even "I didn't mind him or her," it appeared as though The Quest would not be fulfilled. Finally, one friend stepped forward.

"I wasn't going to tell you about my instructor, because you're not in engineering, but you seem pretty desperate," he said. "The guy I had for graphics was incredible."

We discussed the finer points of learning and teaching engineering graphics, and how his instructor had mapped this territory. I was definitely interested. Still, the class didn't meet any of my requirements. By taking too many classes that did not fulfill any requirements, I would never graduate. I wanted to. The question loomed: To take, or not to take? In the meantime, I started reading my roommate's engineering graphics book.

It was decided, when I learned the class could

actually meet a requirement, as two friends informed me after they changed colleges, from Engineering to Arts and Sciences. They had petitioned to have the graphics class count for their visual and performing arts requirement. And their petition was approved! Upon hearing the news, I prepared a class schedule for the next quarter that included Engineering Graphics I.

Just before I scheduled classes, a friend told me of a great professor she had for her class in fiction writing. On the strength of my friend's recommendation, I rejected engineering graphics in favor of Michelle Herman's Writing of Fiction I. Finally, I would have a respectable professor who had something of value to say. I was delighted. "Life is good again," I told everyone. "The Quest is over."

Six weeks later I received my Approved Class Schedule for Winter 1994. At first everything looked wonderful. I had been admitted to English 265, Psychology 310, German 201, and German 292. Then it struck me. Next to English 265, where it should have listed "M. Herman," it didn't. In its place was "J. Anderson."

The celebration had been premature.

I didn't want to accept it. I informed the people at the English Department that they had made a mistake. No mistake, they told me. Michelle Herman was taking the quarter off—something about being pregnant or having a kid. They had kind words to say about the replacement instructor, but secretly I cursed the child of M. Herman.

As the class unwound itself, I found it leaving much to be desired. The premise was that each student would write a few stories and give copies of those stories to everyone in the class. We would have to read the story and write a full-page critique on it. Copies of the critiques were to be given to the writers, as well as the instructor. I like the concept, but in practice, it fell flat.

To a room chock-full of wannabe writers, Judy Anderson provided no guidance or direction in the art of short story writing. Each day proceeded the same way. The students would come in and comment on the stories that were prepared for discussion that day. As the forty-minute mark neared on the discussion of any one story, Judy Anderson would give her reactions, often a summation of what the students had come upon with minutes earlier. And this was the extent of her instruction.

For some reason, most of the stories ended up covering similar topics. Perhaps since the first few stories involved major issues, such as divorce and suicide, the students felt compelled to continue in this vein. Over the next few weeks, we read of the plight of one mother kidnapping her own daughter, and of the suffering homeless man who dies on the street, and of the despair of two people wanting to marry but unable to.

I decided to break out of the mold for my story, to do something a little lighter, have some fun. I told the tale of two guys who drive to Dayton in search of their Rock N' Roll goddess.

~ ~ ~

Ryan Forsythe
English 265
Judy Anderson
Story #1

Slack and Me & the Quest for Kim Deal

My friend Slacker called to remind me that, as per usual, I would be the one to decide the entertainment for the weekend. Slack always deferred his vote in any matter requiring thinking processes.

His real name is Jeff, but the last time he was called that by anyone other than his mother or teachers was back around fourth grade. Even his old man calls him Slack. We all call him Slacker because of his laid-back approach to anything and everything: school, work, his parents, even girls. Slack once had a date with Shannon Collins. Somehow he could just not bring himself to leave my house in the middle of *Star Wars*. I realize it's his favorite movie, but he could've at least called and said he'd be late. Instead, we stayed up and watched the whole *Star Wars* trilogy. Personally, though, there's no way I'd skip out on Shannon Collins.

"I'm waiting, Al. What's on the agenda for the evening?"

I figured I'd stick to the tried and true. "What say we do the usual?"

"Nah," answered Slacker. "I think we should do something fresh, exciting, dangerous!" That actually was the usual response from Slack. He always wanted me to come up with some exciting idea, but somehow we managed to find ourselves at Biff's Billiards every weekend. We had a neat arrangement whereby he'd bring the vodka or schnapps and I'd bring the o.j. We'd get hammered out back, before going in for some really wild pool.

"Besides," Slack continued. "We're seniors now, man. It's time we start finding some college women! Unfortunately, the beers at the Revolting Cocks concert cleaned out the wallet. And, I forgot to tell you, but my father found my fake I.D."

"Perhaps you'll learn from this," I intoned, a la Slack's mother. "You should really spend your time in a more productive manner than hanging out at the arcade. You could put more effort into your classes. Maybe a job would motivate you—"

"Hey, man. I don't make fun of—well, I guess I do make fun of your mom. But you know how sensitive I am about my family. If you're going to mock someone, there are plenty of people in your family you can knock."

Slack was certainly correct in that my family has quite a varied assortment of characters. My aunt Ruth likes to send me every article in the newspaper that mentions Notre Dame, except of course if it mentions they lost some sporting competition, in the hopes that I'll go there next year. So far I'm unconvinced. It's not so bad that my mother prepares bodies for showings at the Melbourne Funeral Home over in Greensburg. What is so bad is that she will only talk about her work over dinner. My father appears the most normal in the family to outsiders, but we all think he is the weirdest. He doesn't talk! In my family, it is just not normal to only speak when spoken to. My father, however, has mastered this. Of course, the cast of my family's unique personalities would not be complete without telling of myself.

It's my last year at Taylorsville High School and, contrary to my aunt's beliefs, I do not plan on continuing onto higher education. Me and Slack plan on forming a rock group. I have been practicing singing (in the shower, though, so my folks don't suspect anything). I've put aside five dollars a week for the past two months from my busboy job at the Denny's over on State Road 46. In another two months, I'll be able to buy a guitar. The cool thing about that is that I can practice all I want without my parents knowing: I can't afford the amplifier for another eight months. But that was my intent for the future.

"What to do tonight, Slack? Now that you've lost your I.D., what should we be up to?" I asked the question, knowing I'd have to come up with the answer myself. I had never needed an I.D. myself. When Slack perused the shelves of our Indiana liquor stores, he was generally quite protective of his beloved New Jersey driver's license. I guess it was inexcusable, though, to think he would always be careful with it. He seemed so proud of it, though.

While he waited for me to be inspired with a wonderful way to bide our time, Slack related the story of how his father "found" his I.D. "Remember last Tuesday, Al, when I told you I had to pick up my brother at the library? I was driving by the Shop N' Go on the way and there's this new sign in the window that says something about 'Mad Mondays: Save fifteen percent on all beer'!"

"But it was Tuesday, Slack."

"I'm getting to that. Don't jump ahead. Anyways, I stop and pick up a twelve of MGD and as I'm setting it on the counter, I think to myself, 'Whoa. It's not Monday.' But as I'm already at the counter, I figure it's like a sign, so I go ahead and buy it. I got so toasted, I actually showed my dad my I.D. He was cool and stuff, though. He said I could have it back when I turn twenty-one."

That was definitely Slacker.

"Hey, Slack! I just remembered something that made my day when I overheard it in math today. What say we take an adventure?"

"Road trip! Count me in."

I could always count on Slack to agree thoughtlessly to my ideas. Just as long as I drive and pay for gas, he has no qualm being, as he liked to be called, "Radio attendant, first class."

"I overheard Archie Neuhe in trig class today say that the brother of a friend of his cousin saw Kim Deal at a mall. Can you imagine running into Kim Deal at a record store?"

Kim Deal, former bassist with alternative rock superstars the Pixies, and currently singer/guitarist with the Breeders, was the consummate rock star, as far as I was concerned. Slack was not nearly as moved by her efforts as myself, but he was still appreciative of the music.

Knowing of my affections for Miss Deal and her abilities with the guitar, Slack knew how I wanted to spend my Friday night. "What are we waiting for, Al? Let's go find you your Pixie."

When I informed him where the mall was located, though, Slack was less than receptive. "Dayton? Isn't that in Ohio? I don't know, Al. Sounds like it could be dangerous."

"Oh, come on. It's not that far over the border.

What better way do you have to spend the evening?"

"Yeah, but Ohio?" Slack remained unconvinced. "What if the cows trample us?"

I had to promise him that we would not be trampled to death by a roving pack of mad bovines. He finally relented when I reminded him that we were much closer to Hicksville than anyone in Ohio.

"Oh yeah," he said.

He was sitting on his front porch when I arrived in my rusting '81 Pontiac T1000. What a piece of work. Two thousand pounds of scrap-metal held together by three rolls of duct tape and a quart of elbow grease. Slack laughed as he hopped in the car. "The Chevette From Hell rides again."

As we turned on to new State Route 3 heading north, I pushed the car up to 54 miles per hour. It's kind of neat, being able to know what speed you're going without looking at the speedometer. Actually, I had better be able to tell the speed, as the speedometer increased exponentially while the car's speed increased arithmetically. But my car could only go fifty-four before it would shake vigorously and parts would fly off. As we turned onto 70 East, we were on the edge of losing the side-view mirror: pushing fifty-five. It was mine, though, and that's all that mattered.

Slacker was still kind of iffy on the whole Ohio

thing. "I think we're hunting in the wrong place, man. She's probably on tour or something. Why would Kim Deal be hanging with a bunch of cows, anyway?"

"I don't understand the problem. You didn't have this problem when we went to Cincinnati for the Pixies show. What's the deal? And about Kim Deal. She doesn't now, nor has she ever, nor will she ever hang with cows. Don't talk about the woman I love that way. And I don't think she's planning on touring until Summer. I heard something about her doing the Lollapalooza tour."

Slack apologized for his indiscretions regarding Kim and cows, but shared my excitement regarding a possible Summer tour.

"Ohio: Welcome to the Heart of it all." It was rather dark out, but Slack was able to read the dim white letters on the blue sign as we passed underneath, before adding his own personal commentary. "It's not too late to turn back, Al."

"But we're having so much fun."

I figured a little driving music would put him at ease. Reaching under my seat, I pulled out the worn black cassette case and passed it to him. "What tape do you want to listen to?"

"I would say it's getting too dark to read these but I have them memorized." Slack ran his finger along to the third one from the top. "Since you are in hot pursuit of Kim Deal, we'll play some 'Here Comes Your Man.'"

"I was hoping you'd say that. Kim will surely be in hot pursuit of me when she sees these wheels!" We laughed at the possibility of anyone, let alone Kim Deal, finding any interest in my T1000.

When we got to the mall, it was a few minutes after eight. We still had almost an hour to look for our favorite Pixie, but the parking lot was relatively empty. "Hey, Slack. What kind of car do you think she drives?"

"Probably a Rolls Royce. All those big star types drive limousines. I think it's part of their contracts."

"You're wrong, man. She isn't going to take a limousine to the store when she goes on a beer run. I bet she has a Porsche." We drove around the parking lot a few times looking for a Rolls Royce or a Porsche or any car that had the mark of being driven by Kim Deal.

No luck. The few cars left in the lot seemed to scream to us: "We are not driven by Kim Deal. Come back some other time to see Kim's Rolls Royce."

Disappointment crept in as it became more apparent that we would not see her. "Don't worry about it, Al." Slacker tried to console me. "Our trip won't be all for naught. We could check out the record stores."

I parked the car and we walked in. Not a very fancy place. There were some rather large plants near the entrance, but this was just a typical mall.

"Are you sure Archie said this mall? Maybe it was another one. I mean, I'm sure she doesn't just hang out at one mall. I guess you and I hang out at one mall, but Taylorsville is a bit smaller than Dayton."

"It was this mall, alright. He said she was spotted leaving a National Record Mart. There it is."

We stared wide-eyed at the store entrance for a minute, neither of us wanting to ruin the moment. We had made it. This was the place where Kim Deal, former bassist for the Pixies, was seen coming out of by Archie Neuhe's cousin Heather's friend Stacy's brother Bob.

Wow.

Slack broke the silence. "Let's check it out."

We walked carefully around, inspecting the various sections. Somehow we were drawn to the alternative rock section, perhaps by the unseen, but still felt, aura of Kim Deal.

I picked up the Breeders disc "Last Splash." Kim's picture graced the back of the box. "Slack, this is Kim Deal today. See how happy she is. I think it was wrong for us to try and find her. Finding her could totally disrupt her life. Maybe she'll be composing a song in her head and we'll come along, whooping and hollering "It's Kim Deal!" and she'll just lose the beat. We could be the downfall of the next Breeders album. I think we should go before we destroy her career."

I put the disc back in it place and turned to go, but Slack stopped me. "You're wrong, Al. I think it is now necessary that we find her. You're doubting Kim's need for a strong base of fans. The constant abuse she probably takes from her fans is probably like therapy. She needs us to find her and try to disrupt her life. That's what keeps her a normal rock star."

Slack's explanation made sense to me, but it was still time to go. The cashier's voice told us there were five minutes left, although his eyes seems to say "I hope they leave soon" and "I could sure go for a cheeseburger."

We bowed our heads upon leaving Kim Deal's National Record Mart forever. Slack had to use the john so while I waited, I perused the big blue phonebooks that hung limply from the payphones outside the restrooms.

While waiting for Slack, it occurred to me that Kim Deal's number might be listed. Slack appeared as I flipped through the D's. "Deacon... Deagall... Deagan... Deaks. Here's the Deals, but there's two K. Deals listed. What do you think, Slack?"

"Your call, man. I'm just in charge of the radio."

"I just have one quarter. I guess we'll have to pick one. Wish me luck."

I quickly dialed the first of the two K. Deals.

"What's happening, Al? Is anyone answering?"

"Shhhhh. There's no answer. Wait, I'm getting an answering machine."

"Hi! This is Kelley, and no, Kim Deal does not live here. I'm not home at the moment, but if you want to leave me a message, leave your name and number, and the time and day that you called, and I'll try to get back to you as soon as possible. Thanks. BEEP."

I hung up the phone. "No dice, Slack. Her name was Kelley."

"Maybe you're right, Al. We just don't seem to have the force on our side today."

Solemnly, we walked back to the car. I started the engine and was backing up when Slack nearly scared me to death.

"Wait!" he shouted before opening the door and running out.

"What the hell are you doing?" I yelled to no one at all, as he was already at the mall entrance.

He was back in two minutes and handed me a page from the phone book.

"What's this for?" I inquired as I noticed all the names starting with D. The thought suddenly struck me. The address for the second K. Deal could be Kim's.

"Slack, you're a genius!"

We pulled into the 76 Station off the freeway and asked for directions to Caribou Road. The attendant did not seem too knowledgeable in the ways of rock and roll, but we placed all of our trust in him. The little man with the pinstriped shirt and the red face said to go down Main about three miles, take a right at Cecilia Ave, take that to the fork in the road, follow the left road another couple miles, until Velouria Lane appears on the right, and take that all the way to the end, which will be Caribou Road.

I would find my Kim Deal yet.

We only got lost four times. Each time we devoted ourselves religiously to the instructions of new gas station attendants even though they could not fully comprehend our Mecca. Seventy-Six turned into Super-America, which in turn turned into Lou's Gas Mart.

Eventually we found ourselves at the end of Velouria, looking east and west at Caribou Road.

"There it is, Slack! Number 900." We stared at the two-storied lime house, wondering just what we would find at the house of K. Deal. This had to be the house. We could not have come all this way in vain.

"Shall we, Al?"

"I believe we shall, Slack."

After parking the car, we made our way up the front steps. I'll admit, I was nervous the first time I stood on K. Deal's front stoop.

"Um, Slack?"

"Yes, Al."

"Do you know whether it's proper etiquette to knock or ring when at a home you suspect to belong to a famous rock star whom you've never met before, even though it could be just a regular person's house?"

"Can't help you with that one, Al."

"Just wondering."

We decided finally that it would be more appropriate to ring the bell. Knocking on someone's door is a personal thing, sometimes requiring one to open a screen door. We decided it would be best to ring the bell, since we had never even sent fan mail to Kim (as we had never known her address before, since we had never driven to the bathroom at the Dayton mall before).

After a quick depression of the bell, Slack turned to go. "No one's here. Let's go."

"Slack. We came to see Kim Deal. Let's at least wait and see if she's here before we scurry off."

Slack and I were both holding our breath as the door swung open. I think we were relieved in a way when we were greeted not by Kim Deal, but by a young man with greasy hair. He was wearing a green flannel shirt and appeared about twenty years old.

"Can I help you?" he inquired, then belched, his lips showering the stench of alcohol upon us.

I spoke. "Um. Is Kim Home?"

"She ran to the mall," he answered flatly. Even

though he seemed in a happy mood, I was surprised when he offered me a can of beer.

"No thanks," I answered, noticing the strange label on the can. Slack's old man would have a fit if he found out we accepted something un-American. "Buy American," he always told us. "Even with beer."

The drunken lad shrugged off my refusal, implying an answer of "Suit yourself."

We must have looked so foolish. The two of us standing on the porch of this person we had never met before, never spoken with, not saying a word. But he had said this was Kim Deal's house! Of course, how many Kim Deals are there in the world? I tried so hard to think of something profound to say. And though I'm embarrassed to say it, I stood on Kim Deal's welcome mat and my mind was a blank. It really was not that intimidating of a welcome mat, but under the circumstances, I think my reaction was justified.

"What do you think, Slack? Should we go?"

"Listen, man. We came here for a reason. We won't be able to face those guys back at school if they find out we stood on Kim Deal's porch and just turned to go. I think we should wait."

Somewhere in the night, a garage door opened. A pair of lights flashed across the porch as a '78 Malibu pulled up the driveway. We watched in silence as the midnight blue car with a dented maroon fender disappeared into the garage. The garage door closed and with the exception of the small amount of light coming from inside the front door, Slack and I were bathed in absolute darkness.

From the back of the house I heard a voice. It was definitely her. The melody I heard was like flights of angels singing beautiful songs for my benefit alone. I looked over at Slack, wondering if he felt the power of this moment. I did not think he did, but I dared not speak.

"Hey, Kim. There's two guys at the front door, want to see you."

"Are they salesmen, Bro?"

"I don't think so," Bro answered her, before belching again. Turning to us, he inquired, "Are you salesmen?"

We shook our heads no, and I wondered just what fate befell salesmen who dared ring the bell at the Deal house.

Suddenly, the door opened further, revealing her presence. Her hair hung loosely over a marvelous green pullover, as she stood there in the most amazing faded blue jeans. We were blinded by her brilliance. Or perhaps it was the light from the now-revealed kitchen which pierced our eyes as we stood on the darkened porch. Slack and I fell to the ground, bowing our heads before the goddess of music. Yes, Slack could feel the moment, too.

When she spoke, every word was magnified. All background sound ceased to exist. We heard none of the cars that passed by on the street, nor the hum of the electric street lamps. We heard not the wind that whipped through the trees, nor the dog that howled in the night. All that mattered to our ears was Kim.

I knew that if my life were to end right then, it would have been a full life, when her voice sparkled through the air. She said, "What the fuck are you doing?"

It was pure magic.

I stood there, trying to think of a proper response. I was not real positive what had drawn me to the home of Kim Deal. Perhaps I was there to be prompted to greatness as a rock singer in my own right, to receive the musical baton of inspiration from the only person that I could ever accept it from. Perhaps I was there to determine whether my rock goddess was indeed like the God that I learned about in the Saturday morning church classes I attended all the way through seventh grade. Sister Anna Marie taught us that God was both fully divine and, in the form of Jesus, fully human. As Kim Deal stood in front of me in her human form, I could testify that she was indeed fully divine.

Although I kept these thoughts to myself, I did reply to her question. She might not have thought it an adequate answer, but I thought it more than explained what we were doing. I replied, "Believing."

We stood up, and Slack turned and walked down the steps. Before she could react, I gave Kim a quick peck on the cheek, turned around and followed Slack. As I was getting to the bottom of the steps, I thrilled to her voice sparkling through the night air yet again.

"Keep the faith, man."

As she said the words, I felt my knees start to buckle beneath me, but I managed to make it back to the car alright. As I put the car into drive, I thanked Slack for joining me on this most special day. I honked as we drove past her house, wondering if she would forever remember me and the brief time we shared. Probably not the same way I would remember her, but in love, you have to take risks.

Not wanting to soil the memories of our minutes with Kim Deal, we drove the whole way home in silence. In the time I had to reflect, I realized that there are two types of people in this world. On the one hand, there are those that just cannot comprehend the power and significance Rock N' Roll has to our earthly existence. And on the other hand, there are Slack and me.

~ ~ ~

For the most part, class seemed to enjoy the story, as noted in both the class discussion and the critiques handed to me afterward. Jenny Queen wrote, "I really, really, really, really liked your story (4 reallys)." Probably the most favorable response was from Brendon Hanley who began, "CRITIQUE of 'Slack and Me and the Quest for Kim Deal' (otherwise known as: the greatest title for any story every workshopped at this university)." He went on, "I must confess: here I was late at night settling in for my beauty rest. I figured, 'Hmmm, I'll read the two stories that I have to read for English 265 with Judy Anderson and those'll put me to sleep...Frankly, its after four o'clock in the morning and I am ready to go rock somewhere. I'm ready to go find all of those idols that I have wanted to meet my whole life."

Yes, the class received "Slack and Me and the Quest for Kim Deal" quite favorably. But Judy Anderson...not so much. I believe her term for it was "pointless." She broke from her usual routine and spoke out after only twenty minutes of class discussion. Students had been sharing their favorite parts with each other, when she spoke.

"Do you mean to tell me, class, that you think

this, this little story, is the greatest thing you've ever read?"

Considering the impression the tale had made on my classmates, I was disappointed. Even moreso when I received the grade. It's unfortunate that the class could not give the mark. What bothered me most, however, was seeing how other students had been graded in comparison.

The class sat in a circle, and I usually sat to the instructor's immediate right, peering over her shoulder at the grades circled on the students' papers. Yes, I admit I was being nosy, but I'll just blame my curiosity. As I glanced at the grades for each student, a pattern began to develop. Not every one wrote about life-changing issues. Those who did, though, received very high grades, just about all A's. Students who, like me, decided not to concentrate on the serious subjects, received solid B's or worse.

That's not to say that I think the former deserved lower grades. I had a different kind of story, not necessarily a better one. If two students can write equally well, and they put in similar amounts of effort, perhaps there is no reason they should not end up with about the same grade.

Thinking about this grade difference impacted the writing of my next story. Do I write the campy fun story I wanted to write and risk getting low marks?

Or do I deal with truly meaningful issues and cement that "A" for myself?

I started writing the "A" paper. By the end of the first page, Alan had come home to find Shannon's body alongside a suicide note. I had consulted friends in pharmacy to make sure whatever pills she had taken would be lethal, and to find out what they looked like. It was at the end of that page, however, that I realized what I was doing. Not something I wanted to do. So I stopped. Instead I started writing my story, about the writing of that suicide page, and what lead me to it, and how terrible it was. In my attempt to strike revenge on Judy Anderson, I wrote "Writer's Block," detailing Paul Forristal, a budding author whose publisher, Justine Andrews, doesn't allow him any freedom to be creative.

He has signed the contract without reading the fine print. It turns out, she can dictate the content of his story or he would not get paid. He grapples with the question of writing her cheese-filled Movie-of-the-Week or not getting paid.

~ ~ ~

Ryan Forsythe
English 265
Judy Anderson
Story #2

Writer's Block

-for me-

Closing the door behind me, I knocked the Cleveland slush off my boots inside the door and plopped down on the sofa. Checking the mail, I was not too pleased to see a big manila envelope peeping out behind the numerous bills. Manila often instilled a deep fear in me. It was usually the sign of a rejected story, returned from the various magazines to which I shopped them around. A glance at the return address on this package, however, revealed that it was from my own publisher, the Andrews Publishing Company. The initial reviews of my first book had finally arrived.

After a few deep breaths, I emptied the contents of the envelope over the coffee table. I don't know how other authors handled these things, but criticism and I never got along famously. Perhaps my perfectionist tendencies contributed to this lack of intimacy with the reviews.

The first one pleasantly surprised me. Harold Brenner, well-respected book reviewer for the *Washington Post*, was quite generous with the praises. The last paragraph clinched it for me. I read it aloud. "Through the wildly entertaining *Blueberries and Bologna*, Paul Forristal demonstrates that he is the most talented new writer today. Though it maintains a comedic fantastical element, his debut is both honest and believable. I eagerly await more madcap adventures from him."

The next review was similarly complimentary. Janet Bishop of Cleveland's *Alternative Press* noted, "Forristal's delightful first attempt is a runaway success. His *Blueberries* is deep in feeling and deeper in humor. The dawning of the age of Forristal is upon us."

I could feel myself beaming, as I read through the stellar critiques. This was simply incredible. While each review was not equally as flattering as far as the subject was concerned, nearly every critic mentioned strong writing.

The last paper in the stack was a note scrawled by Justine Andrews, my publisher.

"Hi Paul. Congratulations on the reviews. Looks like *B and B* is a smash. I'd like to talk to you about a few things. Give me a call or stop by the office tomorrow. Thanks, Justine."

I couldn't wait to see what Justine would say.

The next day, Justine was business as usual, her shaky eyes staring out from behind that massive oak desk. "Well, Paul. You are under contract for three books; you've given us one. I know you haven't been working on a story lately, so you really need to get moving. Ideally, we'd like to have the next one out by the end of the year, while you're still fresh in people's minds."

"That only gives me nine months..." I didn't believe what I was hearing. She didn't even mention anything about the reviews. "*Blueberries and Bologna* just came out, Justine. Don't you think—"

"Save it, Paul. It's high time you learn the reason this company is able to maintain such a high profit margin, the reason we're able to pay you as generously as we do."

"What are you talking about?"

"Do you really think you deserved a three book deal, and for that amount no less, with all those bonuses, based on the fact that you had a few stories published in two or three local magazines?"

Admittedly, the amount of my contract was rather large in comparison to those received by others I knew. But an author needs enough confidence in his own abilities to believe a hefty contract is most deserved. My work was loads better than all that crap populating the market. So while I was somewhat surprised by the terms advanced by the Andrews Company, I felt I was worth it. I figured they saw how great my work was, and rewarded me with the healthy stipend. "Are you saying I don't deserve the contract I received?"

"Now don't think that we don't have every faith in your capabilities as a writer. We have the utmost respect for your writing, Paul. However, undiscovered talent does not necessarily translate into a hot commodity. If no one knows your name, the books are not going to sell."

I sat speechless, not really sure I comprehended what this had to do with my book. With the exemplary reviews garnered by *Blueberries*, people were starting to know my name. And with reviews like that, people would certainly start to buy the books.

Justine continued. "Our staff maintains a high level of involvement in the story process. We generally let an author run free with his first story, mostly to reassure us of his ability in writing. If we're lucky, he'll attract a small following.

"To be blunt, Paul, we do not want another comedy from you. We think you do have an incredible knack for writing, that can be better suited to writing melodramatic stories. Besides, your brand of subtle comedy does not translate well into movies."

"Movies? What the hell does that have to do with anything I'm doing?" I shouted. "I'm not writing a fucking movie. I am trying to write something people find entertaining, something people enjoy reading. And, as you can tell from the reviews, I have done just that. Now, if there is nothing else you have to tell me, I am going to go and write my book. And, Miss Andrews, I'll be damned if I let you dictate the kind of book I write."

"Perhaps you should consult your contract before you go around damning yourself, Mr. Forristal. If you read the very fine print of our little agreement, you'll note that we can and will dictate the level of involvement our editing staff takes in your books."

"No. This is not happening. There's no way I'm under contract to write whatever you and your minions want."

"Check the contract, Paul. Page three, section seven. You'll find something labeled 'Clause A2.' The clause dictates a few creative liberties we may take. I suppose you'll be consulting your lawyer now. Close the door on your way out."

I called Bob from the car phone and explained all the details of my conversation with Justine.

"I don't even have to check the contract, Paul. That sounds about right. Yes, I remember. I didn't really understand the clause at the time, but she pretty much has freedom over the content of your book."

"Why the hell'd you let that slip? Why didn't you say something?"

"I figured after they saw how brilliant your writing was, they would have no reason to introduce it. And after I saw all those zeroes, I certainly wasn't going to quibble over a few measly clauses. You have to admit, that was a pretty good chunk of money."

"So I'm screwed. Isn't there anything I can do?"

"I suppose you do have a couple choices. We could try to fight the legality of the contract, but I've gone over that thing a number of times from a number of different angles, and the thing is solid. You could just try to get out of the contract. Occasionally a company will release someone from an agreement if it's clear they don't want any part of it. The company fears the person won't put forth any effort and the company loses in the long run from having a few lethargic souls. I think this company of yours is going to be less than receptive to this approach."

"What do you suggest?"

"I suggest you write their story. From the standpoint of the contract, you may have no choice. And you only need to do two more books. After that you could go wherever you please, write whatever you want. Write the book. Then take the money and run."

"I really don't believe this is happening."

"By the way, Paul, great book! My wife and I both loved it."

The next morning I stopped at Justine's office to discuss just what I would be doing if I did decide to write this story of hers. I wasn't sure what I'd do, but I wanted to understand everything before weighing options.

As I sat down, she didn't even look up. Staring at her pen, twirling it in her hands, she started up with the movies again.

"You just don't understand the importance of marketing a quality screenplay."

"I don't need to, Justine. I don't make movies."

"For the screenplay, it's important that you include more description of the characters, what they're like. The production company needs to know what they are like when they go to cast them. Don't take this the wrong way, but your weakness has always been describing the characters. Sure their dialogue is great, but who are they really? What kind of clothes do they wear, how old are these people, I need to know stuff like that."

"But this is a book! Why do I need to know about screenplays?"

"Listen, Paul. These days, if your book cannot be easily adapted to a screenplay, you might as well find yourself another business. Now that you've come back,

I guess I can explain just how we do manage to be so successful."

She detailed her side business, shopping screenplays to the major television networks and movie studios. All the screenplays had been adapted from the books published by the Andrews Publishing Company. "When the movies are successful, people are inclined to buy the book. If the book is successful, the studios are inclined to buy the screenplay. It's a win-win situation, Paul, and you can be a part of it."

I honestly could not believe what I was hearing. Justine wanted me to sacrifice my art, my livelihood, my comedy. And all for financial security. Worse than the fact that she offered it to me, was the fact that I considered it.

"Melodramas are what sell, Paul. Comedies don't win academy awards. Nobody wants to see comedy in a movie of the week. The people want action, adventure, intrigue. They want heartbreak, romance, drama. People want to experience danger from the comforts of their living rooms. We can give that to them. And don't you even try to tell me you can't write decent serious fiction. I've read your magazine shorts. If you're a good writer, you can write anything. And you are a good writer, Paul. But don't worry. For your next story, we've already prepared the setting, the plot, and the characters. We want to make your transition to this style of writing as smooth as possible."

Perhaps I wouldn't mind writing their story too much. Ideas were always the most difficult aspect for me to create. Once I had a plot, the rest just flowed forth from my fingers. Here I had the plot in front of me. Of course, it would mean giving up my precious humor. I did not know if I was quite prepared to do that. "I really need more time to think about this, Justine."

"Take a few days and think it over. I'm sure your decision will be in the best interests of everyone. But realize, Paul, we really do need to get going."

I went straight home after our chat. Should I let the staff dictate where my story goes and take credit for it? I do get a thrill out of seeing my name in print. But a main motivation in my becoming a writer was seeing the reaction I had on others, seeing that I had some impact on their lives. I didn't really care how people react to the ideas of a board of editors at the Andrews Publishing Company.

Of course, I thought, the public may prefer this style of writing from me. Maybe I would become even more successful. And my lawyer had a good thought. If things didn't work out, I could just do the two books and then be gone. After fulfilling my contract, I'd find a new publishing company. Of course, the next one would require a little more investigation than this one. Maybe a new lawyer. In fact, I could continue to write on the side, while doing Justine's will.

I gave in. Not without reservations, but I would do it. I would write the story that they wanted me to. Maybe I was really a greedy bastard deep down inside. No, I knew myself better than that. A large part of me did not really want to do it, but I was just too sick of all the crap I had put up with to care anymore about fighting.

I called Justine's secretary and scheduled an appointment for the morning to discuss my book or movie or whatever the hell I would be doing.

"I'm glad you've come around to see our perspective on this, Paul."

"Yeah, yeah, yeah. Let's just discuss the story."

She proceeded to tell me that two television networks were planning on doing a Sunday night movie next spring relating to suicide. If she could get my book out by early December, we could shop around the premise not only to the other television network but if it was really well done, the major motion picture studios might be interested as well. Since time was limited and it would only be my second novel, Justine felt we should concentrate on readying the screenplay for the television audiences.

If we got rolling though, we could take it all the way.

I met with the staff to discuss the story. As they explained the inner workings of the plot, I found I actually liked a number of the ideas. Mainly I liked it because I thought it would make a great comedy. Unfortunately, it was supposed to be part action, part drama, part love story.

The story was about The Amazing Stuart, a performer, who spends his life at monster truck competitions. Between pulls, he packs himself in a small box with a stack of dynamite and proceeds to "blow up." His home life is a wreck, though. His children are embarrassed by their father's occupation, and after he was on the road for too many months, his wife leaves him and takes the kids. He doesn't think it's worth it to go on anymore, and tampers with the structure of the explosives in his box, so it will kill him instead of just destroying the box. Of course, his beautiful blond assistant realizes what he is doing and risks her life, saving him at the last minute.

I found it completely ludicrous.

Justine, on the other hand, strongly believed in the story, and not only for its artistic merit. "Think how exciting the explosion scenes will be," she said. "And how wonderful it is when Stuart finds true love in his assistant at the movie's finale. I can't wait to see what you do with this, Paul!"

I dreaded writing this thing. Justine's staff treated me well and were always ready with an idea of which way to go with the plot if I got stuck. I had to keep reminding myself that I was writing a serious piece of fiction, and not the usual satire. This further impressed upon me that it was just not my story.

Every weekday of the following few weeks continued in the same manner. Monday through Fridays, I spent my days working on the "novel-by-committee" and my nights researching the technical aspects of the story. I'd always been the type who found it necessary to clarify all aspects of a story. For some readers, a point in a story that contradicts a fact in reality can invalidate the story's reality. And so I researched. I researched any and all aspects of monster truck competitions: the timing of events, the layout of the arenas, the duties of the various personnel involved, on and on. Most importantly, I researched the effects that a large amount of explosives had on a person crouched in a wooden box.

The writing was depressing work. It doesn't seem like it would be so bad, but taking a noun and verb from Justine and giving her back a sentence, just took all my energy. Of course, it wasn't that structured; it just seemed like it. Writing had lost its reason, its purpose, its fun. I would have called it quits, but I found the research somewhat fascinating. With the story writing requiring no thought, I was able to funnel all the energy I had into the research.

The subject that interested me the most was the explosives. There are several isomeric derivatives of Trinitrotoluene, commonly referred to as TNT, and the least powerful one was the one used by the performers at truck competitions and rodeos and so forth. This type of TNT could be geared to explode in only the direction of the fuse. By setting the explosives in one corner, the blast would take out the two walls nearest it. The other two walls would be splintered away as the first two exploded out, but the performer would be relatively unharmed, a few bruises maybe, but no major damage.

After a few weeks, even the research started to lose its value. I began to realize that no part of me wanted to write this story. I didn't care for the money, I didn't want my name attached to it, I didn't want to learn about monster truck pulls, and I particularly didn't want to see this on TV. Regurgitating the ideas of Justine Andrews was not how I envisioned my career in books.

There was really no reason to be writing the story. I was a mess. During the week, I couldn't sleep, and would end up irritable, pissed at Justine, myself, the world. I was completely exhausted on the weekends, and slept all day, which didn't make me feel any better. My eating habits went to pot. I'd order a pizza while I was up late and would have leftovers for breakfast. And I hated myself for doing all this. I was miserable.

During my fourth week constructing *The Amazing Stuart*, I was sitting in my kitchen when I got a call from an old friend. Michelle Henderson was the chief editor of a short fiction magazine that had published a few of my stories.

"Hi, Paul! I wanted to congratulate you on the book. I think it's absolutely hilarious, and I see *The Plain Dealer* thinks so too. Keep up the good work."

"Thanks, Michelle. That means a lot."

We chatted a little about the book, and she noted that she was a bit worried when she saw the publishing company on my book. "I see you're with Andrews, Paul. I wanted to make sure you're doing alright. How are they treating you?"

"Fine, fine," I lied. "I'm doing alright, really. Why do you ask?"

"Being in this business as long as I have, I've met a hell of a lot of people, and let me tell you, Paul, I've heard a number of awfully strange things regarding that place. I suppose you would know better than I, though.

"What have you heard?" I asked.

"Just rumors. The grapevine says that in some cases the editors over there are so much a part of the writing process they practically write the books themselves. Can you believe that? I don't know how anyone can have any artistic integrity if they let their publisher dictate every move they or their characters make. Having read your book, though, I can see it's definitely vintage Paul Forristal, so maybe I'm way off. Still, I was wondering how you're doing. It's been so long since we chatted."

I remembered when she published my first story. Michelle was the editor at *East Sider Magazine* and published a short I had written, aptly titled "Knee-Deep in Existence, Wallowing in Twinkies." The story detailed the philosophical meanderings of a midnight raid on the refrigerator. Michelle really liked the part about the deviled eggs.

That story had already been rejected by eight or ten magazines, before I submitted it to the *East Sider*. Each magazine replied the same way. They all thought it was a cute little story, but somehow thought it lacked some deep meaning to allow it be published in their deep and meaningful magazines. Then I sent it to Michelle, and she thought it was great. As far as she was concerned, her readers wanted to be entertained and this would most certainly entertain them.

As I submitted more stories, and Michelle published them, a friendship developed. Through the years, we'd had numerous discussions on my stories, other people's stories, the reasons for writing.

And now six years later, her calling reminded me of those reasons.

Michelle was right. I was not contributing to the wonderful world of literature as I had set out to do when I finished college. Instead, I was creating a movie of the week in bound form.

When did all this sour? Five weeks earlier I was the Up and Coming Artist (UCA) in the weekend variety section of the *Lakeland Gazette*. And now, there I was sitting at the kitchen table, with my head propped up in my hands. Glancing up from the table, I noticed the reviews of my book hanging on the refrigerator.

I walked over and read my favorite, the one from Gary DeSanto of the *Jersey Examiner*. "*Blueberries and Bologna* is a humorous story about growing up, the likes of which I haven't seen in years. Forristal is on fire with this comedic tour de force. Another gem like this will catapult him to the heights of genii."

Sitting there with my reviews, I remembered why I had written the book that I had. It was not spurred by greed for riches or critical acclaim or any of that good stuff. I wrote it for myself. All the stories I had ever written, were written for me. They helped me get through everything from relationships to sheer boredom. Hell, I wrote "One Up On Doody Myers" just to keep me awake while camping out to buy tickets for the Monsters of Rock.

But all of them I wrote because I wanted to write them. I did not care to impress others. Granted, I did get a lot of satisfaction when others appreciated them, but that was never my motivation. I wanted to write for me. I couldn't let anyone take that away from me.

But I had. I had let Justine Andrews dictate the story I would write. All the critics wanted to read more of my own work. Unfortunately, I could not give it to them. I had signed my soul over to the devil for an easy life. I sold out. I wouldn't be able to face anyone after they see my name on *The Amazing Stuart*. What would Michelle think? I knew that I simply could not go on living like this. I would be pretending that I had authored this book, when really Justine would be using my name to sell a few more copies. It is a startling revelation when you find that you're a phony. But there I sat full of the knowledge that my life had become a lie.

I could really empathize with that Stuart, though. He couldn't tell people what he really did for a living, because it was an embarrassment to his two daughters. Sure, he could tell people after the family leaves him, but then what's the point. I couldn't tell Michelle the truth. Maybe I do have some integrity somewhere within, but what good is it unless I use it. What good is creativity, imagination? Nothing if one does not utilize them. That made up my mind. I knew what I had to do.

Unfortunately, I didn't have a lovely assistant to stop me.

First I wanted to make sure Justine knew that I would never again write another line for her and her lousy company.

Returning to the office the next morning, I told Justine that I could no longer do her evil bidding. "I really can't do this, Justine. I never wanted to be a writer like this. It's destroyed me. I can not in good conscience continue supporting you and this greedy little thing you call a business. Consider this a termination of my services."

"For your knowledge, there is no way out of this contract. You won't be able to have your pathetic comedies published by anyone until you give us two books. You have no choice but to fulfill your agreement."

"Is that so?" I responded, as I turned toward the door.

Justine softened, and tried to get a similar reaction from me. "I'm sorry I snapped at you, but I really feel you should think this over a little more, Paul. I'll give you a few more days. Just don't make any rash decisions. Just let me know what you're going to do."

I nodded, "I'm sure you'll be hearing from me."

As I sit in this box, my head is ready to burst from these and a thousand other ideas. And so I guess it will. Before I end this, though, I have a few more thoughts.

As far as authors go, there are many who would say

it is necessary that I mention where I got the dynamite, or the fact that it was the most highly explosive of the many derivatives of TNT, or where I set up this box. They would say it is important to list countless other trivial facts and details. While that may be important in writing an effective short story, that is no longer important to me, for I no longer consider myself a writer. A true writer would not sacrifice his creativity for a free ride. I suppose this is important not just in writing, but in life. It is important to follow one's convictions, to figure out what is the right thing to do and to do it.

Anyways, I'm kind of in a hurry. I want to do this before Justine goes on her lunch break.

Goodbye cruel world,

the Amazing

Paul Forristal

The explosion was heard four blocks away in the second floor offices of the Andrews Publishing Company. Justine Andrews, the company's president, looked up upon hearing the sound, but decided it was nothing and went back to what she was doing.

The End

~ ~ ~

Like me, Paul initially agrees to the offer. He starts to research the manner in which the main character plans to destroy himself. Ultimately, he decides that he can't write what she wants him to write, and so, rather unlike me, he blows himself up.

Coincidentally, my story happened to be the last workshopped for the term. This would be my statement, my way of saying, as I walked out of her class forever, "Take that, Judy Anderson! I'm not going to sacrifice myself for a grade."

When she walked into class that day, she did not take her usual seat next to me. "I'm going to sit across from Ryan today," she announced. "So I can give him the evil eye."

She knew what I was up to, not having to look far to find the meaning in the story. Everyone looked at me. What's she going to do to him, they whispered. I'm glad I didn't write it, they thought. I sat tall, though.

The discussion began and most students admitted really enjoying it. One student noted, "There are so many little details that just add to the story. Even the dedication works well." There at the top of the first page, it simply read: "for me."

Only one student seemed to miss the boat on my purpose. "I only had one problem with it," he said. "I didn't get a good feel for Justine Andrews; I'd like a physical description—"

"Like we all don't know exactly what she looks like!"

It was Judy Anderson herself that interrupted. The student stared back at the instructor. Suddenly a wave of realization flashed over his face. "Oh," was all he said.

And what was Judy Anderson's response to my condemnation of her?

Class ended as it always did, with her providing her comments on the story of the hour. "I'm sure you're all wondering what my thoughts are," she said, glaring at me. "Well...I loved it."

The collective jaw of the class dropped.

She explained herself: my story spoke of the trials and tribulations, the hardships of being a writer; the inner turmoil of deciding whether or not to sacrifice one's art; the suicide—these were all serious issues I was dealing with.

Of course she loved it—I had done it. I had written her after school special.

I received a little satisfaction when I got home and read the critiques from my fellow classmates. Knowing that Judy Anderson would receive copies of all, I was caught way off guard by the honest reactions of my classmates. The first one I read made me laugh. "This story manifested such a jarring level of symbolism," began Amie Tschappat. "It certainly motivates one to attend the class discussion."

Another student noted, "I think this is a great story to end class with, sort of a final remark." Dagfinn Senturia did not like how my story ended with the author dying and Justine Andrews going about her business. "This ending Justine or Judy wins in a way," he wrote. "She's destroyed another writer either way."

I'm not completely cynical when it comes to higher education. Despite these bad experiences, I do feel that the concept is a good one—that education is probably necessary in order for a society to progress. A number of these classes provide background and preparation for students wishing to pursue interests in these areas, whether that be through working or further education. The General Education Curriculum of the College of the Arts and Sciences outlines the philosophy:

In setting out on the life-long road of learning, students must do more than simply acquire a range of facts about humanity and the universe. They must also be encouraged to discover the relationships and significance of those facts—to recognize a problem, its elements, and its implications and to bring it into a clear perspective that encompasses a wide variety of approaches and solutions.

I find this a most noble aim, to help students learn to develop skills and abilities in a variety of areas. However, the curriculum at many schools has the negative effect of including students in certain classes who would rather be anywhere else. Rather than a pleasant assortment of would-be biology majors, the class overflows with students who can't, in fact, stand the instructor's repeated use of a two-word expression, and remain in the class for no other reason than the simple fact of it being required.

This is not to say that I will depart from five years in the world of higher education having learned nothing. On the contrary, I've gained a number of invaluable experiences. Few of them have come in the classroom. Perhaps my classroom experience has been limited largely by the fact that many of the classes I took, I had already taken.

For some reason, the Honors Department at Ohio State believes there are certain classes that are more difficult than others for everyone who takes them, regardless of whether the student has seen the material before. In order to receive those two extra words that

I wanted on my diploma (actually six: "with Honors in the Liberal Arts"), I filled out an Honors Contract, indicating the classes I planned to take until graduation.

My plan would be reviewed and if it appeared difficult, I would be approved to graduate *with Honors*. It was understood that a program containing numerous honors courses, science classes, and upper-level classes, would be easily approved. For example, calculus and physics and chemistry are considered more rigorous (unofficially, of course), and therefore more likely to receive approval, than geology or astronomy or algebra.

In high school, I never learned about geology or astronomy. I was too busy studying physics, and integrals and derivatives in my calculus classes. Unfortunately, I skipped over a few classes to get there. Mr. Knight decided I would do well in A.P. Calculus, so I never saw a day of Analysis or Advanced Mathematical Topics as other students had. At the time I thought it was great: I could actually get college credit while I was taking my high school class.

But then I went to college and found out that, just as I had in high school, I had bypassed other, possibly more interesting areas of mathematics, and landed right in the middle of calculus. The biology and physics and chemistry courses, which I took to improve my chances of getting that designation, were similarly a rehash of high school material. Buying my physics book my sophomore year in college, I found that it was the exact same book I had used two years earlier in high school. Some may say, "Great, easy quarter?" I just wondered what was the point? I skipped half the classes. I didn't care. And so I got a worse grade the second time I saw that material.

While evading physics and chemistry problems that I had already seen, I could have been discovering all about geological science or poultry science or agronomy, or any of a large number of things. Others may say I would have been bored or that I would still hate my professors, but, at the very least, it would have been new material. I would have been forced to read the book and actually learn something. For each of my physics exams, I studied a total of one hour. I got decent grades. So what? I say. I didn't learn anything. I guess I did get something out of it, though. A few words added to my degree.

I shouldn't degrade my desire to graduate with Honors. Who wouldn't want their diploma to bear a mark labeling the recipient as distinct, somehow special? I wouldn't mind sitting in my office in a few years and hearing visitors as they glance over my shoulder at the diploma on the wall "Wow!" they'll say. "You graduated with honors. I'm impressed." Maybe it's like a vanity plate. My own personalized degree. Everyone's has their name on it; what's so special about that?

How sad that what others will view as a mark of academic distinction, I will see as an act of conceit.

Is it really my fault for wanting that designation, for wanting a diploma that says I graduated "with Honors," so much that I took useless classes with unimaginative instructors? Yes, I guess it is. I could blame Rosemary Gliem, who as my advisor four years ago, informed me that I would certainly be frowned upon should I take Entomology 100 instead of Chemistry 121. She isn't my advisor anymore. I could say it is the fault of instructors who bored me to the point of doing play-by-play on their behavioral quirks throughout class. But really I am to blame. Somehow I knew going in to half those classes that I would get nothing out of them. And yet, I took them.

Yet, I didn't choose the instructors. Maybe I shouldn't have been in those math classes, the physics and biology classes. Maybe I should have been learning about something different, something new and fresh. Somehow, though, I think I still would have been bored out of the back of my skull if the instructor in any class said "in fact" 119 times in one lecture. So partly I think I am not to blame. Even if I took other classes, does that mean the instructors would have dramatically improved? Supposedly my honors classes were taught by the better professors. Doesn't that mean that if I did take the other classes, I'd be *more* disappointed?

So who is really at fault?

Quite simply, I blame myself for desiring a designation more than an education; however, I hold the university responsible for providing such a poor quality of instruction, that I could even consider the thought that five years and thousands of dollars has bought me little more than six words on a paper.

Ryan Forsythe
The Ohio State University
Class of 1996
"With Honors in the Liberal Arts"

Kim & Me

I wrote "Slack and Me" and "Writer's Block" for English 265 at Ohio State, during winter term which ran January through March 1994. A week after the course ended, I was driving past the Newport on High Street in Columbus. And there it was: "Breeders." Kim Deal's band was coming to town.

I rushed out and bought tickets. And then I printed out a copy of my story. No way I'm going to the same building where Kim Deal would be without a copy of "Slack and Me & The Quest for Kim Deal" to hand her if I got the chance.

So there I was at the concert, ten-page story bouncing along in my back pocket. I went with my friend Archana, who lived in the dorm room next door, and my brother Bob, down from Cleveland for a visit.

Opening acts were the Faith Healers UK and the John Spencer Blues Explosion. I had never seen Blues Explosion, but my brother and I enjoyed how John Spencer occasionally punctuated the silence between songs with shouts of "Blues explosion!" To this day, it is still possible to hear us shout out the occasional "Blues explosion!" at random times throughout the year. Thank you for that, John Spencer.

The Breeders delivered a fine set, including the hit single of the day, "Cannonball." It was good to see Kim again after becoming a Pixies fan during what turned out to be their farewell tour. Yes, I went to see U2, but came away having seen opening act the Pixies. Soon I had most of their albums. It was some months later, after *Doolittle* had become my new favorite album of all time, that I learned the Pixies were no more. Kaput.

At the close of the Breeders show, we hustled around back, to the spot of land between the building and where the tour buses sit. And we waited.

It wasn't long before Kim's twin sister Kelley came out. Most of the forty or so waiting fans rushed to the building entrance, begging her to sign things. But we hung back, closer to the tour bus. After ten minutes, she had made her way to us. Kim still hadn't come out yet, so Kelley stayed chatting with us.

Archana and Bob raised their eyes to me, then to

my pocket, indicating I should pass Kelley the story. But I hushed them.

Kelley asked who was on Bob's shirt and he told about the comic book character Death being reincarnated every 100 years and this time, she's a punk rocker type (*see back cover picture taken that night*).

Again, Bob and Archana urged me to give Kelley the story. "Dude, it's her sister. She'll give it to Kim."

I stood my ground. "This is the Quest for *Kim Deal*," I told them.

After ten minutes chatting with Kelley, she wondered what the hell the rest of the band was up to, and she disappeared back into the building.

A few minutes later, Kim emerged. We still hung toward the back of the crowd, near the tour bus, but after a few minutes of signing ticket stubs for those immediately near the building, Kim turned to go back in. I saw my chance slipping away.

I rushed through the crowd, story high in hand, shouting, "Kim! Kim! I wrote this story about you! Kim!"

Just at the doorway, she turned and saw me at the bottom of the stairs. "Yes?"

Out of breath, I shouted a nonsensical "Iwrotethisstoryformyclass, it'sabouttwoguys…"

She came down the steps, grabbed the story, looked at me and said, "Thanks, I'll read it on the RV."

And then she disappeared back into the building.

Woo hoo! Goal accomplished! Though the story doesn't end there.

On our way back to the dorm on north campus, I told every stranger I passed that I had met Kim Deal and that she had my phone number. Because let's face it: you don't hand Kim Deal your story, with the possible chance that she would read it and fall in love with it and therefore you, without a way for her to get in touch. Duh.

ABOUT THE AUTHOR

Ryan Forsythe is currently a student at the Ohio State University, majoring in English and Psychology. Inspired by his neighbor Archana, who met Kim while working at the Amar India restaurant in the Dayton area, "The Quest for Kim" has been his crowning achievement as an author. As for the future, Mr. Forsythe would be thrilled to no end if Ms. Deal were to read his story.

If Kim does ever read this and would like to contact the author, he can be reached by phone at 1-614-293-7520 or in writing at Taylor Tower Room 918, 50 Curl Drive, Columbus Ohio, 43210. Of course, she should also feel free to stop by anytime.

(By the way, for anyone wanting to reach the author now, do note that the contact info as been out of date since June 1994.)

Heading north, we crossed High Street at Woodruff, near Larry's bar. Just as we were getting to the West side of the street, Archana heard a voice somewhere in the night and started to say "That voice sounds just like—" At the same moment I was glancing over my shoulder at a woman in a green jacket. I said, "That is—"

We stood and watched as a group of bouncers from the Newport hustled Kim into the bar directly across the street from where we stood, before the bouncers turned and headed back south to the concert hall.

We looked at each other for one second, already knowing our next step. Immediately we crossed High Street again and headed into Larry's.

Before we could spot her, we found a table and sat down. But then I saw Kim at the bar. "Wait here," I told them and hopped up.

Walking up behind Kim, I noticed my story, folded in half (giraffe, not elephant) sticking out of the pocket of her green windbreaker. I decided to go for faux suave. "Excuse me, Miss," I said in my best Cary Grant. When she turned to look, I added, "But that's my story in your pocket." I may have winked.

She smiled. "Hey! Yeah, did you say you wrote it for a class?"

"Why, yes. Yes, I did."

"What grade did you get?"

I decided not to mention the initial grade that Judy Anderson had given my paper, and instead go straight to the re-grade.

"I got an A."

"I'm an A!" she said.

Just then Archana appeared at my side. "Hi, I once served you water at the Amar India restaurant in Dayton."

Kim looked at her and thought for a moment. "I was only at that restaurant once. But I remember you. You were nice."

While Archana beamed, Bob appeared in his black t-shirt. Taking a look at the shirt, Kim asked, "Is that Kelley on your shirt?"

Bob again told the quick tale of Death's centennial reincarnation, this time as a punk rocker chick.

We all thought it odd that she thought it might be her identical twin sister gracing the shirt, but not herself, one of the most important women in alternative rock history, but we didn't point this out then.

After a few more words, she kindly excused herself. "I'd love to stay and chat, but I have to get back to the band." She motioned toward the pinball machine.

As Kim wandered away, I noticed she sported a Rolling Rock beer in each hand. We wandered back to our table, but I was soon back at the bar to pick up drinks.

Turning from the bar with a Rolling Rock in each hand—if it's good enough for Kim, it's good enough for me—I was surprised to see a familiar face. Brendon Hanley!

Yes, there were about twenty people in the bar—half of whom had performed on stage that night; in addition to Kim, members of the Faith Healers UK and Jon Spencer Blues Explosion hung around the pinball machine. But one of those kicking back with a few beers was the very person from my English 265 class who had read the story at 4am and was ready to go find his rock idols (*see page 45*). The very person who wrote in his critique, "I guess you could say that, in a way, your story is an inspirational one for me."

If Brendon's was not the most complimentary critique, then surely the honor would go to his roommate Jerry. In fact, two of the reviewers in "Writer's Block" represent these two, Harold Brenner (Brendon Hanley) and Gary DeSanto (Jerry DeCicca). Yes, that's how thinly veiled that whole thing was (there was also a Janet Bishop in the story and a Jenny Queen in the class).

Seeing Brendon so soon after I gave Kim the story that he professed to love, a story that was now sticking out of Kim Deal's pocket in the very bar in which we stood, I felt some sort of cosmic karmic destiny thing going on. I started shouting like a crazed asshole. "Brendon! Oh, my god! She's here! The quest for Kim Deal! The Quest is complete! I gave her my story."

He saw the Rolling Rock in each of my hands and the dazed crazed excited look on my face and assumed I must be bombed out of my gourd. Which only made me try harder to convince him that I hadn't had any alcohol yet, that I wasn't crazy.

"I'm serious! She's here. I gave her the story! She's playing pinball!"

"Okay, sure thing, Ryan. I'll catch you later." He wandered back to a table with some friends.

After I sat back down with Bob and Archana, I noticed the seat Brendon took was facing my way, but happened to be between me and the Taxi pinball machine. And out of the corner of my eye, I noticed him noticing me out of the corner of his eye. He noticed me eyeing the pinball machine. And I saw him get an expression that seemed to say "Well, it doesn't hurt to look."

Turning for a quick glance at the Taxi pinball, Brendon froze. For there stood Kim Deal. He turned back and looked at me, then again at the pinball machine before excitedly telling the story to those at his table. He pointed my way and the table turned to look. I raised my beer. Yes.

Brendon went home that night and told Jerry, the other person in class who loved my Kim Deal story moreso than any of the other poorly written amateur class writing projects. Jerry was the one who just before our class discussed "Writer's Block," came in and told me he had visited Judy Anderson to discuss his own story. And he asked if she had read mine. He told me she just stared at him and scowled "Yes." One minute before Judy walked in to that class, Jerry said, "She got it all, Ryan. Gooood luck, man." Judy understood everything.

After class when I read the one-page critiques, Jerry's leaped out at me. It seemed that he thought I might follow the lead of the Amazing Paul. He wrote words to the affect of "If I am a better reader than most, and this is the end, then I will dedicate many stories to you, my friend."

But no, I wasn't about to kill myself over a few fun little stories. If you're out there, Jerry, I hope you weren't disappointed at my lack of commitment to the story.

Months after the Breeders concert, I bumped into Jerry and he told me a story. He was at the Newport for the Guided by Voices show, and he spotted Kim standing near the mixer table. He felt stupid asking, but he had to find out about the story. Had she read it?

Jerry approached her and asked if she remembered receiving a story at her show back in April.

He told me she was either really stoned or really stupid, because she just stared at him for a few seconds, like he wasn't there. But then, a wave of realization.

"Oh, yeah! I remember that. I read that."

Jerry told me that the dazed look immediately returned, end of conversation. But before they parted company, she did light his cigarette, which he saved for me. He told me it was on his dresser and whenever I could come over, it would be there for me.

I'm not sure why, but I never stopped by. And now, years later, I'm out on the West coast and Jerry is back in Columbus. I haven't seen him in all this time, but apparently he fronts a band called the Black Swans (if I can trust my Googling skills).

I wonder if Jerry ever tossed out that cigarette. Or does he still hold on to it, as a marker of the day we received confirmation that the Quest was truly complete: not only had we gotten her the story, but Kim Deal had indeed read—and remembered—"Slack and Me & The Quest for Kim Deal."

A Final Note

A year or so after class with Judy Anderson, I petitioned to take the Creative Nonfiction class in the graduate MFA program in creative writing with Professor Bill Roorbach. As I recall, he said something like "My mother's maiden name is Forsythe! Sure I'll let you in!" So it was pretty much me the undergrad in with a bunch of graduate students. Judy Anderson was not in my class, but as a member of the MFA program, she could have been. Still, just about all my classmates would have been her friends and/or colleagues.

For this nonfiction class, I wrote "Five Years and You're Out" (though I submitted it without including "Slack and Me" or "Writer's Block" as presented here). Similar to when my fellow undergrads were required to comment on whether they liked the story "Writer's

Block"—and it's message railing against their very teacher—this meant my classmates had to discuss whether they liked the nonfiction piece "Five Years." And it's section railing again their colleague.

Let's just say it made for an interesting class discussion.

About the Author

Ryan Forsythe grew up in Cleveland and attended Ohio State University before traveling extensively, including work aboard ship for an around-the-world voyage. For four years, he and wife Kaci ran a hostel in Redwood National Park. Today they make their home in the woods of the Illinois Valley of South-western Oregon with one dog, five cats, two boys, and no more rabbits.

Ryan is the author of *Dick Cheney Saves Paris: a personal and political madcap sci-fi meta- anti- novel*, *The Little Veal Cutlet That Couldn't*, and *If You Don't Read This The Terrorists Will Win*. His short works have appeared in *A capella Zoo*, *Jersey Devil Press*, *Le Scat Noir*, *The Pacific Crest Trailside Reader*, *Rat's Ass Review*, *The Rogue Valley Messenger*, and more.

Other titles available from Left Fork

- ☐ **Goldilocks and the Three BARs** Ryan Forsythe $8
- ☐ **Cobra Lily: a review of southwest Oregon Literature & Art** $12
- ☐ **Ravenwood** Michael Spring, ilustrated by Deb Dawson $15
- ☐ **10-Year Old Creepy Poems** Rory Forsythe-Elder $6
- ☐ **Slugdala! 13 Banana Slug Mandalas** Ryan Forsythe $10
- ☐ **P4** K. Elder $13
- ☐ **Bicycle Lotus** Sara Backer $10
- ☐ **Here From Somewhere Else** Judith Arcana $10
- ☐ **Unfolding the Field** Michael Spring $16
- ☐ **Come to the Edge** Ruth Rhodes, editor $18
- ☐ **Magician's Secrets** Kailen Forsythe-Elder $8
- ☐ **The Doodle, Design, & Draw Book** $7
  for Illinois Valley Kids of All Ages

All these books are available from your nearest online mega-retailer juggernaut machine, or they can be ordered direct from the publisher. Indicate the number of copies required and complete the form.

Name ____

Address____

____

Send to: Left Fork Books, PO Box 110, O'Brien, OR 97534. Please enclose remittance to the value of the cover price plus: $3 shipping for the first book, plus $1 per copy for each additional book ordered. While every effort is made to keep prices low, it is sometimes necessary to increase prices at short notice. Left Fork reserves the right to charge new retail prices which may differ from those advertised in the text or elsewhere.